good deed rain

This is the author's 57th book.
Others include: *Playground*,
The Wonderful Stupid Man,
The Welfare Office, *Old Salt*,
Violet of the Silent Movies,
Cosmonaut, *Almost Animals*,
and many more...

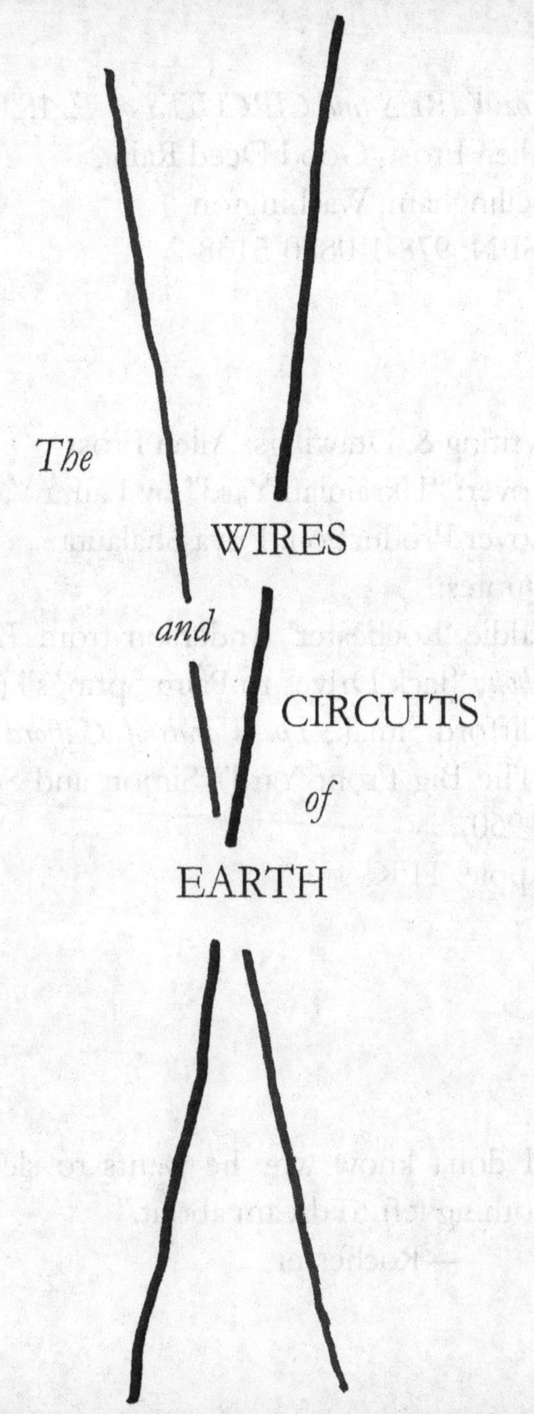

The

WIRES

and

CIRCUITS

of

EARTH

The WIRES and CIRCUITS of EARTH © 2022
Allen Frost, Good Deed Rain
Bellingham, Washington
ISBN: 978-1-0880-5138-2

Writing & Drawings: Allen Frost
Cover: "Ukrainian Yard" by Laura Vasyutynska
Cover Production: Priya Shalauta
Quotes:
Eddie 'Rochester' Anderson from *The Jack Benny Show*, "Jack Drives to Palm Springs" (1956).
Clifford Simak, *The Worlds of Clifford Simak*, from "The Big Front Yard" Simon and Schuster, NY, (1960).
Apple: TFK!

"I don't know why he wants to sleep. He's got nothing left to dream about."
　　　　　—Rochester

The WIRES *and* CIRCUITS *of* EARTH

Allen Frost

Good Deed Rain ◊ Bellingham, Washington ◊ 2022

"once the way was open, then the way stayed open and it was as easy as walking from one room to another"

—Clifford Simak

CONTENTS

INTRODUCTION

I still fool myself occasionally into thinking I can make a living writing short stories the way writers did in the 1950s, sending their creations off to the pulps. This winter I discovered the stories of Clifford Simak [my favorites are: "All the Traps of Earth; Good Night Mr. James; Dusty Zebra; Lulu; Green Thumb; The Big Front Yard"] and I was pretty excited writing mine. I even submitted two of these to magazines. (One was rejected; I never heard back about the other, it may be rusting in some Manhattan inbox). So, let's just pretend some of these stories have appeared in *Thrilling Wonder* and *Fantastic Universe* and you have found this collection at the train station newsstand, and you will bring it wherever you're about to go. Better hurry though, I hear the steam whistle calling you!

1.

A VISITOR in ILLINOIS

The factory was gone, the mall, the monorail was ruined. The city was relying on horses to pull carriages and carts. Like most of America, Waukegan took a few direct hits late in the war. There wasn't much left of it in some places. Those who survived hoped the worst was over. They were afraid to breathe the air out there. If you went outside, you never knew what would happen.

The horse bringing supplies clopped around the rubble piles. People watched from windows or where there used to be windows and a few children followed behind the cart like little birds, pecking at anything that might fall. It was hard to believe not so long ago there were supermarkets brimming with food and now they were chasing after grains of fallen rice.

Then those birds ran from the cart, running with their arms held out. In the middle of them is a girl and her seven-year-old brother. They have a better place to be than behind a government horse and cart. Across the torn schoolyard and the field that used to be a playground was another bombed out neighborhood. Around the burned tail of an air force jet. There was still enough of the wreck to play games on, but they kept to their path, thin and worn as a deer trail between the dry stacks of blackberry thorns and burled weeds until it reached what used to be a street where houses grew. Beyond them, half the city is gone.

"This way," the girl said. Her brother had stopped to pick up a candy wrapper. "That's nothing, we're almost there." They flew up the curb and hopped on each torn asphalt step leading them across what used to be a lawn. "Come on!" She got them to follow her to a bomb crater. There wasn't much to remember the house that used to have this address, a blackened foundation, a tangle of pipes, and the boiler where a Buzzer hid. When the Buzzers started popping up, everyone was taken by surprise, but it was the grownups who started the war. Jenny left her brother with the other kids and went down the crumbled slope.

"Careful," a boy whispered to her. They were

still a little afraid of the Buzzer. Seeing what had become of their city, the lives they used to know, that wasn't unwise.

Jenny never had that fear. She always wanted an older sister and now one had dropped from the stars. It was a miracle like one of those stories she used to read. A week ago she met the Buzzer at the bank of the creek. The Buzzer's long black hair hung over her face, hiding Jenny from her until the Earth girl was close enough to touch her shoulder. She told Jenny she was sad, all alone, she wanted to fall in, she didn't mind being pulled by that slow current out to the sea.

Jenny knocked on the metal boiler door. She wasn't scared. After all, Buzzers and humans weren't that different. This one didn't look like the scary drawings in *The Herald*. The Buzzer really could have been Jenny's older sister.

The Buzzer opened the door and was pleased to see the girl. She couldn't smile but Jenny could tell. Before the Buzzer could speak, she reached into a pocket and got her translator. She didn't have a mouth, but words came through the slim translator device. It was a green stick with a hoop at the top. It looked like the plastic wand from a bottle of soap bubbles, a child's toy, one they used to play with before the war. "Hi Jenny."

Jenny waved. "Hi. Are you busy?"

The Buzzer laughed. What a question—busy hiding inside a boiler in a crater? "No, it's nice to have you visit." She looked up the hill and waved. "And you brought your friends."

Jenny admired the Buzzer's purple cape. It floated around her when she moved. Her uniform was black with green sleeves and she wore a control box belted over her stomach. Buzzers didn't need spaceships. They could travel great distances using their control box. This one was broken though. She had tried to tape it together in the clumsy way a kid would, crisscrossed by scotch-tape like a badly wrapped mummy. She had taken out the broken vacuum tube, if she could find another one, her troubles would be over, she could blink away. Meanwhile, she was stuck in Waukegan.

Jenny wished she could point her arm like that and wave with a cape flowing over her shoulder as she did.

"Why don't they come down here too?" the Buzzer asked.

Jenny shrugged. "They're scared."

The Buzzer made a sound like bees. Sometimes that wand had no translation. She wanted these children to trust her. She didn't want to seem their enemy. She was lightyears from her home and starting to think she might never return. Not as long as her controller was broken, she needed to find that part. That's what took her from the boiler at night, when she would scurry through the rubble looking for a machine that might have a picture tube. Two nights ago, using a Waukegan telephone book, she found the address for a hardware store only a mile away. The Fielding Avenue signpost was bent from some explosion. She found the right spot, but she had to dig to find the shop. So far, the tunnel she made stretched through the doors, past the register. She found a good Swiss army knife but no picture tube. Other nights passed that way, gathering the wires and circuits of Earth technology.

Once, the Buzzer slid into a bookstore. She found a book for children and brought it back to the boiler to read. In the candlelight, a picture of the dark green woods and a little house trapped in the trees drew her in. A crooked old woman lived in there. It gave her an idea. She started to leave

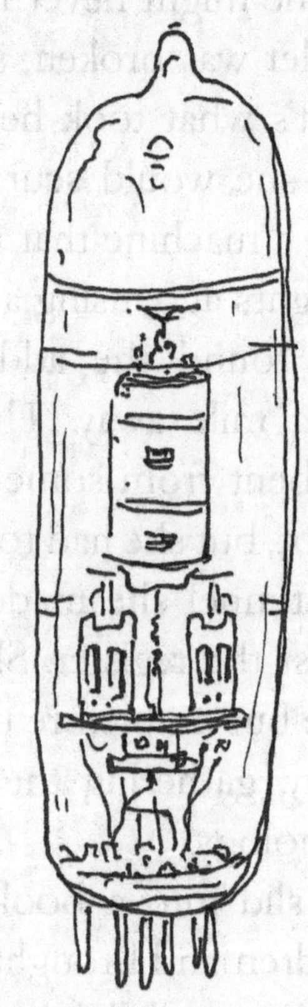

toys and candy and other things she thought kids would like. A couple chocolate bars and a rubber crocodile placed where she had seen them pass by. The Buzzer found another good illustration too— it was all planned with fairytales—when the girl discovered her, staring at the water like The Little Mermaid, she knew she had them, Jenny most of all.

"I'm glad you're not scared," the Buzzer told Jenny. "Look what I got for you." She gave the girl a cardboard box from the Ben Franklin store. A toy was displayed inside, behind a cellophane window.

The girl was delighted, she beamed, you would never know there was a war. "A rowboat!"

"It's remote-control." The Buzzer buzzed. She knew Jenny would help her. The Buzzers were very efficient getting their way. Just look what they did to the moon and Florida.

"Did you check your TV?" the Buzzer asked her.

"Mmhmm." The girl set the present on the ground and searched her pocket for a notebook. She found the latest page and read it aloud, "It's a 1972 RCA, 15-inch screen."

"Black and white?"

Jenny nodded and added, "My parents won't get a color one. They're cheapskates. Now I guess it's too late to ever get color."

The Buzzer was pleased. "And you brought the picture tubes?"

"Mmhmm."

The Buzzer held out her gloved hands excitedly.

"Okay, hang on…" Jenny had another pocket on her coat. The picture tubes clicked in her hand.

"Careful!"

"Don't worry," Jenny said, taking them out, bunched in her hand.

The Buzzer made another bee sound as she read the tiny lettering on the main tube, "15VACp4. This is exactly the one I needed! Oh, thank you Jenny!"

"You're welcome."

"Let me put this in my house. I'm afraid I'll drop it!" the Buzzer laughed. She went towards the boiler and turned and held the wand up to where a mouth would be, "Goodbye!" The boiler door clanged shut.

"What did the Buzzer give you?" called a small voice from outside the crater.

Jenny picked up the box. "Wait until you see!" Her feet made little avalanches of dirt as she ran up the hill. "Come on!" They flew in a bunch like gray sparrows away from the Buzzer's crater and over the playground ruins. Jenny cradled the box in her arms. She didn't want them to know what it was until they got to the pond. None of them had seen a present like this for a long time.

They took turns floating it back and forth. They were still playing with it when Jenny's father found them. It was getting dark. Soon it wouldn't be safe to be outside the shelters. He saw them laughing and pointing at something in the pond, splashing like a turtle. No wonder they were delighted, when was the last time anyone saw a turtle?

He spied on them from an overturned car for another minute, until he figured out what was happening. He couldn't believe it. Where'd they find a robot rowboat? And all those other toys and the candy wrappers they left when they ran. What were they up to? Jenny could make the boat go in circles and backwards and charge with both oars like a duck beating the water. Then he heard them mention the Buzzer. It gave them presents every day. This was the best one yet. When the man heard that, he stood and screamed at them to get away from it. Didn't they know anything? It might be a bomb!

Jenny was so horrified she dropped the control box. It sunk in the orange water. The rowboat scurried for the far side of the pond.

Dusk was falling, satellites would be looking for life. They had to hide underground for the night. They survived beneath the concrete.

Later on when Jenny's father said, "Is it true? Did you meet a Buzzer?" she lied.

"No. I was just telling stories."

After the lightbulb died, when they were on their cots in the black, close to each other, her brother whispered, "Are we going tomorrow?" She told him no, she said she was going alone. She had to see if the Buzzer was still there. But she quieted him, promising him if the Buzzer gave her anything more, she would share. Jenny turned and faced the wall. There weren't any bombs falling above.

Jenny hoped the Buzzer's picture tube worked. At first, she didn't want it to, she wanted the Buzzer to stay longer, but not if her father and the other grownups began to suspect. She knew how her father felt about Buzzers and he kept a buzzgun on the cellar wall.

In the morning, when the lightbulb was on, the rifle was gone.

Flung into the nickel light outside, Jenny ran through weeds surrounding the pond. They made a frail crunch. Before the war, there would have been cattails and blackbirds and bumblebees, blue skies and blue water with the clouds painted on. Somewhere the invisible sun knit itself in the blanket hanging over Waukegan.

Jenny's father tracked her. He carried the loaded buzzgun in the crook of his arm. He never wanted the kids playing in dangerous city ruins, he knew something like this would happen. There were rumors that Buzzers could drop in, set charges and then blink out of sight. *The Herald* had a story about a Buzzer spy, how it was able to disguise itself under bandages like the Invisible Man, like a wounded civilian.

Black smoke piled up from a relief ship burning a mile out on Lake Michigan. Seagulls headed that way.

In her hurry, Jenny didn't know she was being followed. The girl winged across the crumples and wrecks, up the next hill and into the memory of houses and yards and cicadas that churned in June. Then she dropped into a crater.

The boiler door was open.

More smoke smudged to the south. The war wasn't over yet. At night the fires of Illinois lit up the sky.

He wasn't far from them, not close enough to hear what they were saying, but it didn't matter, he took aim with his rifle. His daughter stood right next to a Buzzer, close enough to be its shadow. Getting the Buzzer lined up in the scope wasn't hard, it was an easy target, he just needed them to be a little further apart.

Jenny said, "Does this mean you're going to leave?"

"Yes. I have repaired my controller. I've got to get back, Jenny. I have work to do. But I'll miss you, you've been such a good friend." She hoped it sounded like a fairytale ending. Then she touched a button on the control box and as she dropped her hand, there was a shot. A loud snap and the acrid smell of gunpowder.

But the Buzzer wasn't there. The man on the hill jumped to his feet. How could he miss? He took a step and some rocks spilled down the embankment towards his daughter staring back at him, holding her hands over her ears, eyes like an owl.

0
5
10
15
20
25
30
35
40
45
50
55
MINUTE METER

2

The DIAL

Anyone can buy a time machine. They're stocked at your corner store, in the aisle next to the candy. They started appearing around ten years ago, though it's hard to imagine a time without them. They're as necessary to our daily lives as the Kleenex you can get on the next shelf, near the Band-Aids.

Everyone makes mistakes and would like to change the past, but now when you find yourself at fault, you can just go back and erase it. The product is perfectly safe, you can't turn the time machine dial and travel haphazardly. To prevent mischief they can only go back five minutes. It's so safe they even market them to children. My daughter would love one, but she's still too young. The commercial is repeated between Saturday morning cartoons, that merciless jingle mixed with kids going back in time to get out of chores, or to eat a pie again.

A lot of disasters have been averted that way too. Time machines could be the greatest thing to happen to the 21st century. It keeps everyone on their toes. You can't walk down the sidewalk without someone blipping from sight.

I was headed for 7-Eleven to get one. I was in a bit of a panic too, I only had a few minutes to get there and buy one and set the dial so I could pick up my daughter from school on time. A minute ago, I realized it was 2:30, I had to hurry.

That may not sound like the sort of thing you need a time machine for, but it's not unusual. Ordinary life can always use a little help and that's what they're here for. Like the song on the commercial says, "Keep a time machine handy and your worries are over." Just the other day, I was late to work. Not by much, but I used my time machine and everything was fine. I should have known to buy a replacement. "Always keep one handy and you're fine and dandy."

I parked the car and hurried inside the store. I knew right where they were, I've been here before.

"Hello," I heard the cashier call and I mumbled something back. I wasn't in 7-Eleven to carry on a conversation. I grabbed a Ready Now time machine package off the tine and quickly paced to the counter. Ready Now is the cheapest brand, but they're all pretty much the same as far as I know. They take you where you need to be. As long as it's only five minutes ago.

A man stood at the register talking to the checker. I've seen his kind before at work. They wander in and they need you to know how in-tune with the universe they are and pretty soon twenty minutes have gone by. He was braying about the Mariner's pitching staff. I had to interrupt.

"I'm sorry," I said, "I need to go back in time." I waved the Ready Now. Everyone's been there, everybody knows what that's like. He stopped mid-sentence and stepped aside for me.

I slapped ten dollars on the counter and said, "Thanks! Keep the change."

I'm not a bad parent, at least I don't think so, this was just one of those times I needed to change. These things happen. That's why we have time machines. I checked my watch as I sat behind the steering wheel. I was doing okay.

A school bus passed me on 23rd, loud and bright as a beehive. With any luck, her class was running late leaving their room. On 24th the traffic started, parents wheeling in and out of the roundabout and more buses leaving the lot. I parked in the first space I came to. I could hoof it the rest of the way. I was close enough to hear those little voices chirping ahead.

Glad Anderson Elementary is alive at this time, when all those kids swarm out in rows and they jumble with their parents—the ones who aren't late—and there's that happy sound filling the air.

My daughter was standing next to the teacher, near the front steps. Oh God, was she crying? I had really blown it. I stopped under a tree and scrabbled at the packaging on the Ready Now. I had to tear the cardboard backing to get it out. You'd think they would make it easier for people in an emergency! I glanced at the school again. The teacher had her arm around her.

The Ready Now time machine is just a thin block of black plastic shaped like a doorstop. You can get time machines in a variety of shapes and colors and some of them are made to look like crown jewels, but this is a basic model. It was charged and ready to go. I turned the round dial back five minutes. Then I pressed the red button.

I was spinning in the middle of a shimmering

atmosphere. I felt a little motion sick but I knew in a moment I'd be looking at the school. I would hear the clink of the rope on the flagpole and then the bell would ring and Glad Anderson would be alive again. You don't really have a sense of time unwinding around you, but you know you're in a dream going backwards. Soon you'll wake up. It's weird to think of time like tangled string.

In hindsight I wish I would have just run up to her and let her cry in my arms while I told her how sorry I was and explained to Ms. Magnusson how awful I felt that I was five minutes late. This is the future though—we don't need to do that anymore. There are so many situations that can be avoided now. But look what I've lost using a time machine. I could blame it on the Ready Now, but really it was me, it was me turning the dial.

Like most mass-produced electronics, this one had a malfunction. The 5 on the dial didn't stand for five minutes, not even five hours, or five years for that matter. The Ready Now brought me to the world five million years ago.

DILLY'S GOLD

This is an adventure story, an RKO film starring Humphrey Bogart and George Raft in the cold relentless mountains of the Pacific Northwest. It begins in a house on 32nd Street where Dilly was tired of having things stolen from his garage, and he was tired of the mortgage payment and bills, and he had to take a second job, and he was 72 and feeling it. But he had one final brilliant idea…one that would solve all his problems.

He was waiting for me when I crossed the street. I was struggling with our dog, leash wrapped around my leg as she yawped for the ball I had in my other hand. Dilly wasn't concerned, he kept to his own reality. It didn't matter if I was wrestling with a demon, he wanted to tell me something important. I stopped on the sidewalk and gave the ball to our dog. She invented a game where she drops the ball, I pick it up then she wants it again, leaping in the air.

"Did you plant the rhubarb?" he asked me.

That's when I noticed the blood on his hand. "Yes," I said. "In the backyard." He brought us a box of starters from his garden a couple weeks ago. I dug them into the ground with the dog bounding around me.

"I still have thirty feet of soil to move," he continued.

"Is your hand okay?"

"Yes, I'm fine." He brushed the blood off with his sleeve. "I was cutting roses and they got me."

I had no reason to doubt the roses.

He said hello to the dog and she dropped the ball she was holding and I reached to keep it from rolling in the street and she snapped it up quickly, dragging the leash and me. I pulled her back from the curb and asked Dilly, "Hey, I was wondering about your gold claim?"

It was no secret. Months ago he told me he found gold flakes in a stream out near Baker Lake. He was all worked up about it, he told me he brought two buckets of sediment home and was going to pan through it and he was sure there had to be a motherlode upstream and he was going to find it. He was taking his housemate Ronald and as much gear as they could carry. At the time I wished him well and told him not to let it go to his head when he became a millionaire. He assured me he wouldn't, he promised he just wanted enough to pay off his house and his car and he would give the rest to his family. That was the last I heard of the gold claim. Meanwhile, he still had the same pickup with flat tires sighed next to his garden, he still had the tarp hooked around his chimney. There were no fountains or sports cars. I figured he didn't find that gold. But I was wrong.

He told me what happened.

I didn't know what to say. The dog was pulling me steadily. She wanted to get home and so did I, especially now that I had seen the blood on Dilly's fingernails. I listened to him chatter until I was finally able to break away. "I'll see you," I said as if it was just another ordinary exchange, but it certainly wasn't. Dilly had reached his limit. His eyes jumped about from the road, over to a crow, back to me as his story clattered on.

Their partnership was doomed. Ronald up on the slopes of Mount Baker panning for gold in some freezing creek was hard enough to imagine.

Ronald has been living in Dilly's house on and off for years, getting more frail and forgetful with the passage of time. I've seen him staggering around in the woods, leaning on a staff to take a breath. I couldn't picture him goldpanning in the mountains. How much assistance would he be in those mountains? And how much could he be trusted anyway? He depended on Dilly. But finding all that gold could change everything.

Ronald wouldn't remember where the gold was, you could count on that, but Dilly couldn't take that chance. What if Ronald woke up from a dream, his mind clear as a winter morning, and what if he grabbed a shovel and the car keys and took off? Something had to be done, there was a secret to carry to the grave. Dilly was a survivor. He did what he had to do he thought.

And now Ronald was part of the garden across the street from us. Maybe that same spot where the rhubarbs grew. As the dog and I skittered up our gravel driveway, I thought of Dilly planting Ronald in that deep soil, and I tried not to think of Dilly's eyes as he told me what he had done. We were nearly running for the door.

No, it wasn't like that. I could see it unfolding

that way, and it would have been a more thrilling story, but that's not what happened. Dilly told me the mountains never gave up more gold. What he collected wasn't much, about a third of a vial that shined like the eye of pharaoh, but it wouldn't bring the kind of money he dreamed of. And he and Ronald weren't a match for the hills anyway. They stayed foggy and undiscovered. And now it was starting to rain. So no, he didn't kill Ronald. He didn't need to.

Everyone saw Ronald getting worse every day. There were paramedic visits. I've seen the flashing lights on the street. Dilly had been through it all before with his mother living there, caring for her and seeing her to her end. He couldn't do it again. And last night someone kicked in the door of his barn. He simply had enough. There seemed to be no end. There was no gold, no easy way out. Nothing was more horrific than that. But at least he had his garden, spring was coming, he laughed. Eyes same as they'd always been. After he sifted out the gold, he confessed, he threw those buckets of river silt into the garden soil. He wanted to see if gold would grow on the vines. He was ready to believe they could.

VIENNA CLEANER
OPEN

4.

SWEET DREAMS

Sunny blue sky, a warm breeze made the palms lean, and their leaves scratched at the porch railing where he slept in a hammock. At least in his dream. He woke up and the room was freezing. His wife was curled tightly on the other side of the bed and he could see his breath cloud from him. The blinds let in rays of early white light.

It was just barely spring, two weeks in. He got up, he showered and dressed, he left home for work, but he wasn't going to work. He called in sick. And in a way, he was sick. On the corner of Chestnut Street, he didn't notice that a cherry tree grew from Cascade Bank and it was flowering like a Japanese painting. One of these days he would be a famous magician and his worries would be over. The morning turned sunny, but winter was leaving a cold wake. He couldn't wait to put his hands around a cup of hot coffee, but until he opened the diner door, he kept his hands in his coat pocket.

His friend Sam waited in the window, reading a newspaper at the table. Sam was in on the "sick day" escapade. In fact, he pushed for it. Sam was unemployed and every day belonged to him. He wanted Leo to know the feeling. "Come on," he goaded, "It'll do you good to skip a day." Sam was a fool most of the time, but in this case he was right. It did do Leo good to skip a day of work.

Leo pushed the door open and the warm diner welcomed him. A waitress looked at him and he said, "I'm meeting someone," pointing, "Over there." She smiled. The music was in the middle of a song he recognized.

Sam must have heard his voice. He waved at Leo.

They had a table against the far corner, the windows looked out on the busy avenue and the street people going back and forth.

Leo took the seat across from Sam and they talked the way you would when you haven't seen a friend in a year because of work and schedules and this and that.

A waitress appeared next to Leo and said, "Can

I get you something to get started?"

Leo glanced at her light blue eyes. "Coffee please."

She seemed so happy to see him. Was he someone else? No, she really was happy to see him. Wasn't she? It had been so long since Leo flew in this field. She brought the coffee through the room every five minutes and each time he held the cup to her.

Of all things, for a while Sam and he talked about the last president. That was a conversation that should be run through the machines at Vienna Cleaners on Magnolia Street. Gradually they steered out of it and were talking about Sam's cat. Last year, Sam found a kitten in the field near his house. Someone left it there, people really do that. Someone had to save its life. Sam took it with him, gave it a bath and got all the fleas off and named her Joyce. After all that cleaning, it turned out Joyce was a Siamese cat. Imagine that. Joyce would stare at the air, as if something else was being projected and she would be hypnotized by whatever it was, her eyes like river stones.

"Hello sweetie," the waitress said. "More coffee?"

Leo took a breath. She stood so close to him, her patterned soft cotton apron was near enough to fall into those flowers He didn't realize his coffee was gone. "Yes please." He looked at her face again, just for a second. What else was he supposed to say? He didn't know yet. Maybe she would be coming back. He went to work finishing that new cup of coffee so he'd be ready.

They talked a while about the house Sam wanted to build that was up on a grassy hill, tucked in the apple trees, with a view of the sun shining on the ocean.

Was Leo imagining that girl was taking roads between the tables that would keep her going by him as often as possible? It wasn't long before she was back with more coffee. And of course he said yes and showed her his empty cup.

She laughed. "I love it."

Funny thing was, suddenly Leo felt enlightened. Life had shown him new meaning. He would do anything to finish this cup quickly so she would return. If coffee brought her to him, he would never stop, he would bust a spleen for her. He must have had eight refills before he and Sam were done. He held his hands out of sight and folded the napkin into an origami rabbit.

When he left he could barely keep himself still—his hands shook—but it wasn't the coffee, it was her. Nobody spoke to him like that in years, or glowed beside him like a candle. He really let his imagination run away.

"How about that waitress?" Sam asked him. "She likes you."

"Oh no, I don't know. She was just being nice."

Sam laughed at him.

But he was thinking about her. He thought about the cup she gave him. He and Sam crossed Redding Avenue into the ruins of the old pulp factory and Leo was still thinking about her. That was crazy, wasn't it? They walked along where the steam plant used to be, and Sam was talking about how he used to work there and the electrician who did too. One day the electrician was walking on the catwalk and he noticed a loose valve. Steam was whistling out of it. He reached up to turn it off and his hand dipped into the current. The air was firing out at such a speed and heat that it melted one of his fingers off. The space where it had been on his hand was invisible. He went to the locker room and put on a bandage before he went to the main office and told what happened. The floor manager wanted to see where the leak was. So this poor electrician, holding his wounded hand, took them back to the catwalk and he pointed, "There!" with his free hand. And that's how he lost another finger. Sam laughed, but Leo was still thinking about her.

He didn't even know her name.

Maybe she was just a mirage.

He wished there was another world where they were real.

He thought of dreams. Then he thought of the house he lived in. He remembered his wife didn't believe in his magic. In fact, she wanted nothing to do with it. He would tell people he was "a semi-professional magician." He would do parties mostly. He would make flowers appear from nowhere and it didn't matter. His wife saw him as another cheap Houdini. One time they watched a TV show about Houdini and she got angry at him, something about the way Houdini abandoned his family in pursuit of fame and he drowned over and over in a river and came back again until one day he didn't and that's how he left his wife, stuck with Ouija boards and mediums and no word from him. She transferred all of that to Leo, the whole tragic meaning. "Maybe magicians shouldn't be married," she said. He tried to tell her I'm nowhere near Houdini. He said, "I can't survive on magic. Honestly, I'm as close to giving up as I can be. I do magic nobody sees." So yes, having this waitress notice him was a thrill.

Leo didn't tell that to Sam though. He said goodbye to Sam when they got to his car on Railroad Avenue. Leo pretended it was the coffee that made his words tumble end over end. All he wanted to do was see her again. What if he returned and what if he told her he left her the paper rabbit? Oh, but he was getting ahead of himself—first they needed to get to know each other. Of course.

That might have made sense, but he stopped at the next store window he passed. Bargain Travel Agency. He went in and bought two tickets to Mexico. Imagine that! He pictured palm trees, a sandy beach, another world far from America, far from the cold, just her and him.

On the street again, he remembered the words on the cup he held, the one she kept refilling—*Sweet Dreams*, with a big red heart. Wouldn't that be a sweet dream, running off to Mexico together?

When he did go back to the diner, it was a little later. First, he stopped for a while looking at the cold waves on the bay. A boat scudded in the white caps. He thought about where he'd been and where he was going. He thought about blue eyes and cotton cloth. What would it be like to start life over, with someone who wanted him near, with someone who spoke to him so sweetly? When he did return, the diner was closed. They closed at 2 PM.

He stood there at the door like a dummy. A homeless man leaned on the corner lamppost. There used to be places for everyone, jobs and homes and families and America was a dream that was supposed to keep everyone warm.

U S
AIR
MAIL
11¢

5.

FINDING the RIGHT SKY

Maury Valise takes pictures of sky. He drives with a camera on the seat. The back of his panel truck is filled with catalogued photos in boxes and a big map is taped to the wall. Behind the driver's seat there's a switchboard row of dials lighting up the hollow like portholes in a submarine. He ran the antenna up through the slot in the ceiling. It periscoped out of the roof three more feet then stopped and the hoop on top began to spin.

A faint pinging came from the machine. It wouldn't be long, he didn't have a lot of time, she was on her way. He brought the antenna back down and wrote in his notebook. He had been doing this for years. Ever since they lost touch. How many years? That didn't matter. He was dedicated to finding her and bringing her back to earth. At first he thought gravity would remember her, or she would tire of flying sooner or later, grab hold of a steeple going by if she could. Get tangled in a laundry line on some Iowa hill.

But she never did.

They both worked for The Saturn Circus. He was what they called a roustabout, he cared for the animals and pulled up the tents and the highwire and made sure the safety net was secure underneath. Every night the spotlights swam around the crowd and then all flew down to the sawdust. A big cannon was pulled into the center ring. She held out her arms like wings and her cape sparkled like stars as she climbed inside. One night she was shot from the cannon but never came down.

A rip was torn through the tent, but there was no sign of her landing outside. For a full day, they searched the parking lot, the oak trees, and the cow field beyond. "Gwen!" he shouted until his throat was raw. The circus was due in Missoula the next day, but he wouldn't go with them. They went east and he went west, following her path in the air.

She was mythical. She was a Tin Pan Alley song, aeronauts were asked if they ever saw the flying woman in the clouds, the newspapers ran murky photographs. There were clues—a woman's shoe found on a gravel road, a gold button like the one on her uniform.

Sometimes he caught a glimpse of her. Once he wrote her a message on a barn roof, hastily painted big red letters, "I MISS YOU GWEN!" She went past so fast he didn't know if she saw it.

The years went by. He was looking for something no one else could see. He charted her flight with maps in libraries and measured wind directories.

Maury Valise was an old man. He guessed she must be just as old unless being in the airstream didn't age her. In his dreams, she was always the way he remembered her.

He calculated the speed, trajectory and altitude and figured where she would be at her lowest point.

He drove across America so many times to find the spot he was supposed to be. He was careful to make the net from the softest fibers. He tied it between two telephone poles like a big spider web. The field was perfect, the groundcover made of flowers and weeds, there was a slight breeze from the south. Everything had to be done exactly right if he wanted to catch her.

6

SON of MARS

There are two coffee shops with the same name. I was ready to steer into the first one off 76th Avenue, but my son corrected me, pointing at the other one on 77th. It was a much smaller building compared to the first one, and the sign overhead looked hand painted, not made of glossy plastic and neon. Almost like a black-market copy. I drove us into a tight parking lot. Cars were slipped in like sardines on either side. We have a van and it just barely made it. In fact, I could already tell it wasn't going to work, there was no room to open the doors. I groaned and put us in reverse.

It was funny to think we were placed down in this little scene like a toy car on a toy set. The city crunched around us. I couldn't see any other parking spots nearby. I headed for the lot of a drugstore. Even though big signs warned us this was for customers only, I steered in, stopped, and turned the engine off. My wife said she could buy something in the store, she could use another mask. That's all we do is wear masks these days and we go through a lot of them. So we got out and headed for the gray storefront. It's still winter and they were pushing flu shots and medicines and had signs in the window of happy people on Mars. Anyone could go there if they passed the examinations and got their travel vaccines. Sunny Mars.

The door trundled open and we followed footprints across the linoleum. Those smiling faces in the window weren't in here. The shelves were minimally stocked. They were out of masks. Still, people were milling around sort of dazed, I guess, like us. Nothing is like it was.

We left and decided to take a look around for another parking spot. A crow on the warning sign watched us. Maybe he was paid to do that. We weren't customers anymore.

Believe it or not, we ended up in the same spot as before. Sardined. Our son wanted a moment to gather his thoughts. I couldn't blame him. We still had ten minutes before his interview. When he was ready, we slid out the side of the van.

The coffee shop with the painted sign was busy and warm inside. Right away, I spotted the recruiter. You could tell. Another young man sat across from him and was answering questions. I heard him say he was an Eagle Scout. I don't know if that's helpful or not. It is if you need to tie knots on the morning star. We didn't linger. We went outside again. I don't know, we still had some time, my wife and son led the way around the side of the building.

I never had an interview when I went off to college. I just sent my application and got a letter telling me I was in. Then it was me, alone, shot into the world.

The backlot of the coffee shop was blocked off with a tall wood sectioned wall. We couldn't see over it or through any gaps and I joked that it was a Martian zoo back there. Blue brainees scrambled around and a pterodactyl with clipped wings waited for scraps. Anyway, my son looked nervous and just wanted to walk. So we did.

We crossed the street and there sure wasn't much to see. Offices. Closed restaurants. Dark windows. A man in a suit trailing cologne. Yellow tape strung over doors. We went across the street again, past McDonalds. A sign on the door said: *Closed. Drive-Through Open.* That was a short walk to nowhere, but we found the sidewalk and the coffee shop returned. Our son checked the time. We stood by the car and we hugged him before he left. All this traveling in circles and now he was going to meet the recruiter and then what next, he might be off on his way to their school before we know it. I watched him walk into that handpainted backdrop, then I unlocked our van's sliding door and my wife and I squeezed inside to wait.

I sat behind the wheel with a paperback and read about a walking plant from outer space. It was a good diversion. A half chapter later, I was surprised when the passenger door opened enough to let my son back in. We were all questions for him. He said it was okay, it went well and as he told us how, his phone rang, the recruiter wanted him to return.

We watched him go back. We smiled and wondered, was it good they called him back? He must have made an impression. The recruiter saw his potential. Of course, all these years with him, we are well aware. He was still in high school, it was his last year though, and a new adventure was about to begin. I wanted to be inside to hear what was happening, but all we could do was look out the window and guess.

I remembered his elementary school when I would go to pick him up. I'd stand under a tree, the other parents around on the grass too, and listen and watch the classroom windows until the bell. We all took in the air at that sound, we were almost together again. One by one the classes would come out the door, boys and girls, holding colored papers or pinecone animals. Those days seemed just around the corner really. Time goes by in a flurry. We can't hold it or stop it, we're just along for the ride.

At first it felt like a train shaking the ground. A dull rumble shook the van. The café seemed to tremble and before we could react, a cloud of smoke billowed up from behind the building. It came from that Martian zoo, where a rocket was walled in, a thin flinty looking thing shot into the air, pulling a fierce looking yellow flame and a roar. I only saw it for a second, the car windows were coated in a silt fine as factory dust. I couldn't open my door, there was no room to get out and anyway it was too late, he was on his way to the stars, a soft glow in the sky, oh he was gone.

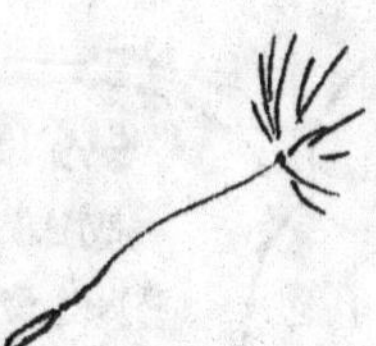

Buôn Mê Thuột
Thơm
Dịu
Đô
Ngon
1269 QUA DUNG DONG
CHO BÉN TRAN
ĐT: 36.201.545
LUWAK
High Quality

7

LUWAK AWAKE!

Louis Luwak is an ordinary salesman. You'd never know he was a fiend. The fact that he sold what he did—made his living from that!—is monstrous. The back seat of his car was filled with boxes of Luwak Awake! and he went from town to town, spreading it like a virus.

I'm one of those people who caught it. I sampled a jar yesterday and I woke up this morning in a tree. I have no idea what happened to me from the time I had a cup until dawn. I can only think Luwak Awake! is some sort of poison or hallucinogen. And if I had been poisoned, was it still in my system, were there more side effects, could I expect it to send me back up a tree at any moment? Now maybe you can understand why I urgently needed to track down Louis Luwak.

It was a miracle I didn't fall. From the branch back to the sidewalk was a twelve-foot drop. I squirmed to the trunk and let myself down with a little help from gravity.

A woman walking a dog saw me and trotted away in the other direction. The dog looked at me over its shoulder and she tugged the leash violently. A strong reaction to a person dropping from a tree.

Fortunately, it was Saturday. If it was a weekday, I would've been late for work. I couldn't tell exactly what time it was from the sun, maybe eight. Maybe ten o'clock. And then it occurred to me, maybe it wasn't Saturday. My arms were sore from holding on. Maybe it was Sunday…or the next Monday was starting over again. That's how out of touch with reality I was.

All thanks to a guy named Louis Luwak, who showed up in my office on Friday afternoon with a briefcase, a sales-pitch, and a free sample. It's diabolical—hitting the offices after lunchbreak when we're at our lowest and we just want to take a nap. He knew he had me when I tried to hide a yawn in my hand. So yes, I had the free sample, and this is where it led me.

I don't even live in this neighborhood. I was blocks away from work, halfway to home.

An old couple coming down the sidewalk towards me spotted me, nudged one another and quickly stepped off into the road. They clung to each other and hobbled into traffic with little concern. Was I so terrifying? What had I done last night? Had I been a holy terror? Did I howl from the rooftops, did I bite parked cars?

I took a chance and approached a man pushing a mower across his lawn. I called, "Excuse me…"

The man stopped and turned towards my voice and didn't seem disturbed to see me. Thankfully.

"I'm looking for someone," I continued, and I described the scoundrel salesman Louis Luwak: his wire-rimmed glasses, the white lab coat he wore over his suit, the alligator skin briefcase he carried, his peculiar gait.

"A lab coat?"

I nodded. "I guess he thinks it makes him look professional."

"He sounds like a kook. Who would trust someone walking around this neighborhood in that getup?"

I shuffled a foot. "Well…" I said, "Regardless of that, some people did."

The man laughed. "I never saw anyone like that around here and if I did, I certainly wouldn't accept any free sample."

"Okay!" I replied defensively. He was no help. I let him get back to his precious lawn. That guy doesn't work in an office apparently, he doesn't know what it's like to be cooped in a room in the golden sun at 2:30 PM with another two hours to go. The blades of his mower paddled into the distance.

At the next corner I slowed to examine the newspaper vending machine. I hoped for some answers, but I didn't expect to see myself cropped into a photograph just above the fold. I couldn't read the rest of the story, but it was me alright, swinging like a sloth from the curved top of a traffic light. Horrible. I imagine my foolish antics gathered quite a crowd. I sighed.

That explained my unwelcome presence in this neighborhood. I was anxious to leave these streets. I didn't exactly know where to find the salesman, but I had a general idea. He lived out of his car, somewhere within striking distance of my insurance job.

Further along, underneath the very traffic light

that had been the sight of my spectacle, I hurried, and the houses turned into stores and familiar office buildings, and I came to the newspaper stand. Sometimes I'll stop by on my lunchbreak to buy a magazine. This wasn't like that though. I was afraid to look at the stream of newsprint. I wasn't worried about *Le Monde* or *The Dubuque Telegraph*, I don't think my antics carried that far, but *The Herald* was another story. I'd already seen a sneak preview in the vending machine. Now I could hold a copy in my hands and turn it.

"Oh no," I muttered. It wasn't flattering. I won't go into the details. I put it back on top of the stack. Next to it was another local paper and there I was again. *The Shoppers Gazette* wanted me arrested on sight! I was "A threat to the neighborhood." They ran an old photo of me from security footage at the Food Giant grocery store. I was holding a pear. The grainy black and white made an ominous picture.

"Hey Looky-Loo, this ain't a library."

A grim bulldog-face leaned over the counter and glared at me. I apologized and straightened the stack for him. I tried to duck into my shirt the way a turtle would as I stepped from the stand

and departed. How had I become the villain when it was Louis Luwak who created this disaster? He was the supplier, I was the innocent victim.

I had to clear my head, I needed to think where Louis would be. I pictured his odd swaggering arrival into the office yesterday. His crooked grin that appeared as I asked where I could find him if I needed more. He was so sure I would want more, he told me he was still in town for another day. Then he would hit the road. He said to look for his parked car. It was a silver Lincoln Town Car. How hard could that be to find in a town full of cars? But there was another important detail. He told me he likes to park near a phonebooth. He said a prized parking spot with a phonebooth was his office. Since crawling out of the tree I had been searching for it.

A rough hand grabbed my shoulder and pulled me out of my thoughts. "Look what you did to my bodega!" I had no memory of the beefy man before me…or his trashed storefront grocery. I was standing on a crushed tomato. He pointed a broom handle at me, "You come back to pay for the damages?"

It was entirely possible I had done this. The

newspapers don't lie. The wooden bins were cracked apart and the shelf that ran along the window had spilled every manner of fruit and vegetable. "I'm so sorry," I told him.

"Sorry don't pay the bills!"

"I know." His hand didn't ease up on me until I reached in my pocket and took out my wallet. Thankfully my rampage hadn't cleaned it out. Who needed money when you're swinging from branches and lampposts? I gave him forty dollars but the crease in his brow didn't go away. So I gave him all I had. Even my lucky Kennedy half-dollar coin.

He stuffed the money in his apron and squinted at me, that broom handle stopped just shy of my chin. He told me I still owed him more and I promised I'd be back with my checkbook and that calmed him down a little. "What's the matter with you anyway?" he wanted to know.

How could I explain? I told him I was the victim of a hypnotist.

I was anxious to get off the busy street, who knows what other damage I could have done? I scraped the tomato off on the curbing as I scuffed over the crosswalk. I wish Louis would have been more specific about where his car was, I would just have to wander up and down the streets and hope I wasn't recognized again. And all this while I was worried that any moment I might revert to whatever state that potion had sent me last night.

I'll admit I looked enviously at the lamppost on the next corner. It would be easy to scale, I could picture going up it so easily. What fun it would be to swing atop. With effort, I drew my eyes to the green street signs bolted midway down, one reading 14th and the other Morris.

Then I remembered Morris Street! Louis Luwak *did* tell me where his car was! My foggy brain had taken this long to unveil that gem. Suddenly I was closing in. Morris sloped to the right towards the river, and to the left it went on deeper into town. Some instinct told me which way to turn. He had come this way before, I just knew it.

Pretty soon I caught a glimpse of the river. Ever slowly, Morris began its slide into that gray water. It was a good location for his car. There were trees along the sidewalk, no parking meters to feed, warehouses and a few small business offices, ones that wouldn't have guards at the door to run off peddlers like him. He just wanted to sell and be gone. He lived a life on the run, he didn't want to be found. I was lucky he told me as much as he did. The giveaway is look for a phonebooth. Look for a location where a car can park anonymously next to one and melt into the shadows.

Across the street, a 7-Eleven appeared. A crumbled tar lot with a seagull on the roof. A phonebooth on the side. I didn't need to climb a telephone pole to look any further.

His car was plain as stone. It wasn't silver, it was gray, worn as a nickel. The windows looked black, tinted to keep anyone from looking inside. It had to be his.

I approached warily. It was wedged under the canopy of an overflowing tree. I got close enough to read the letters on its pitted skin, TOWN CAR, but I had to get even closer to those tinted windows to be able to see in.

He wasn't sitting in there. The front seat was cluttered with maps and paper bags, crumpled wrappers. The guy was a slob. A gerbil would have been at home in there. The seating in back was crammed with boxes. One of them was torn open and I could see the green glimmer of a jar. I never heard of the stuff before, I told him that yesterday, but he promised me it would be everywhere. He bragged how soon Luwak Awake! would be on the shelves nationwide. I hope not. This country already has enough trouble.

I reached for the door handle. Why did I do that? I stared at my hand. Was I tempted by the sight of all those boxes? I pulled my hand back and tucked it under my arm. I hoped the door was locked. I scared myself a little. I stepped back and looked around the thick leaves. I had the feeling he was near.

I was prepared to wait for him. The morning left me tired. I thought of going to 7-Eleven and getting a cup of coffee. Then I could sit next to his car, there was room on the curb under the tree. I wouldn't mind some candy too, something mango flavored. It didn't occur to me that I didn't have any money. I was preoccupied by a new development, something I just noticed.

The trunk of Louis's car was open a crack. I guess that made it suspicious enough for me to open it. I let my hand go. I lifted the lid and there he was. Louis Luwak was crouched in there like a stowaway.

"Oh, hello!" he straightened up. "I was just

looking for something. I'm overdue to Burnsville."
He put on an act, going through the pockets of a
loud plaid suitcoat crumpled on the wheel well.
It had probably been his pillow. I didn't care if
he was sleeping back there or hiding—now that I
found him, I wanted answers.

"You were at my office yesterday," I barked at
him. "You gave me a free sample."

"Yes, yes," he grinned. "How was it?"

"It was terrible! What is that stuff?"

"Why—" he clambered awkwardly free of
the trunk space and explained, "Our product is
nothing less than the very best quality energy
protein refreshment, suffused with necessary
vitamins."

I had to steady his arm as he slid back onto the
cement to join me.

"Listen, Luwak," I steamed, "I don't even know
if I still have a job. I'm afraid what I'll find when I
go back there. I might have kicked over the filing
cabinets and eaten the lightbulbs. For all I know
they fired me!" I wanted my life back. I wanted the
last 24 hours to be gone.

He straightened his lab coat and his voice got
smooth as gravy, "Sometimes—very rarely—

first time users experience complications. But it's nothing to worry about. Now your body has accustomed itself to the exhilarating effects of Luwak Awake!" He reached back into the trunk and picked up a jar, "Would you like a complimentary token of our company's sincerity?"

"No! No. I don't. What sort of complications do people experience?"

"Oh, you know…mild headache, nausea…it soon passes."

"I woke up in a tree!" I blurted. "I have no memory of last evening."

He shook his head. He looked perplexed, "That's odd. That sounds like...Perhaps you had a case of food poisoning from lunch?" He tossed the jar back in his trunk and shut the compartment.

"I was fine until I had the free sample. Then I lost all self-control."

"Okay…" He folded his white sleeves over his coat and sighed. "To be honest, you're the first one to try it. I mean, person. I tried it on a rat, but," he snickered, "it went a little crazy."

"You tested that stuff on me?"

"I had to start somewhere."

I grabbed him by the lab coat collar. I couldn't

stop my hands. They wanted to pull him apart.

"Easy!" he shrieked. "Don't hurt me. I got kids back in Minneapolis who depend on me! Look—" he showed me the picture he kept in his pocket.

"I'm sorry…" I felt bad for him. I got my wallet and it was open before I recalled it was already empty.

"Oh, I can't take money from you. Your decency touches me, honest it does. Here—" he opened the Lincoln's side door—it had been unlocked all this time—"Let me give you this. It's the least I can do for your troubles." He grunted and lifted out a whole cardboard box full of Luwak Awake! He pushed it into my open arms and like a fool, I took it.

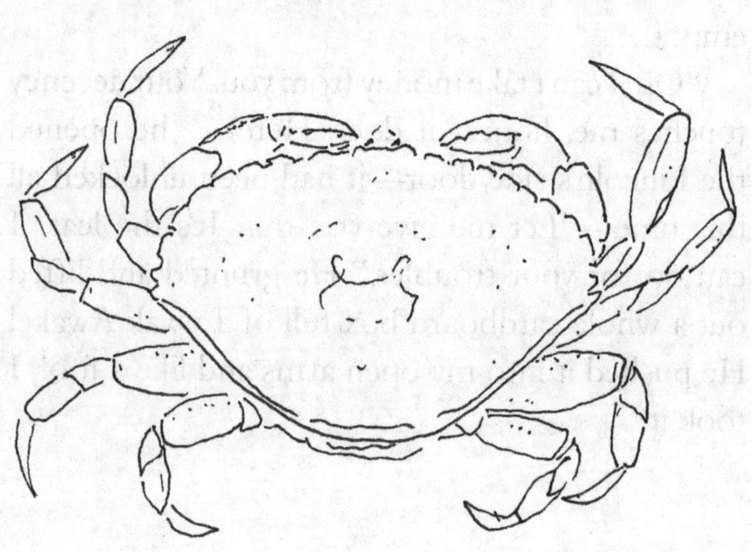

8.

CHASING TELEPATHY

I've been an amateur telepath all my life. Mostly receiving messages. Not terribly interesting probably, like listening to talk-radio. People walk by and I tune in to that. Fortunately, it doesn't last all day, otherwise I'd get no rest. At night they mumble me to sleep.

Foggy mornings seem to increase the range of whatever airwaves they float in. I stepped outside and overheard someone across the border in Canada making breakfast. And the old man in the lighthouse on the point was talking to himself about chowder.

I thought I was going to the coffee shop, that was my plan, but I didn't even make it to the end of the block.

"Help me!"

Her voice made me jump. I turned around. The sidewalk was empty. I thought, "Where are you?"

"Oh, you hear me! Please, I need your help."

"Where are you?"

She told me and I was surprised. She sounded so close, but she was down at the harbor, on the pier. I promised I was on my way, and I returned to my driveway and got in the car. I don't often follow up on the messages I receive. Like I said, I'm an amateur. I don't have the time or the inclination to do this fulltime. Once I helped a kid out of a tree, over on Wilson Avenue. That was easy. I guess it has to be something urgent to make me veer from my routine. She certainly sounded in trouble.

Whoever she was, she had gone silent. I hoped it wasn't too late. I sped along Donovan, uphill and at the top where you can usually see down to the water, the coast was all under a veil of fog. I've heard stories of mermaids out there, everybody has, people swear it's true, and my imagination had me wondering if that's what she was. I don't know why. Funny how the mind works. She could just as easily be pulling my leg.

By the time I got to Harris Street I'll admit I didn't know what she could be. I called out to her a few times, but still no answer. I parked by the old cannery and I let her know again that I was almost there.

The foghorn blew out on Poe's Point. I was in the middle of a white pillow of the stuff. Seagulls I couldn't see were above somewhere, crying back and forth. The smell of the sea clung to the fog while it bristled around me. I almost couldn't see my feet as I left the pavement and my shoes scratched on the boards of the pier. I was as close to running as I've been in years. "Are you still there?" I asked her. My telepathy was out of breath.

"I'm here," she said.

"Where?" I didn't want to run off the end, all I could see was the shroudy figure of a man fishing at the railing. Unless she was clinging to a piling below, I didn't know where she could be.

She said, "I'm in a bucket."

"What?" I stopped. I wasn't more than twenty feet from the guy fishing. He slouched on the rail, a cigarette making a glow. The smoke of it got lost in the fog. I would have too, if I had been smart. Telepathy only goes so far. In front of me was a very old picture, someone fishing from a pier,

with a bucket next to them. Still, a mermaid couldn't fit in a yellow bucket. "You're in the bucket?" I asked.

"Hurry!" she called.

I closed in on the guy and stopped not far from him. "Morning," I greeted him and casually leaned my elbows on the railing.

He replied with a small gray cloud.

I asked, "How's the fishing?" That gave me a chance to lean towards the bucket at his feet.

"Slow," he said and puffed. The cigarette clung to his lower lip.

I was confused. There was a single brown Dungeness crab in the bucket. "Is that you?" I asked her silently. I never had an animal talk to me before. Not this directly anyway, with words in my head. And a crab of all things…

She returned to my mind, pleading, "I will die if I don't return to the water."

Of course that was true. The fate of a crab in a bucket is well known. I thought of accidentally kicking the bucket off the pier and she filled my head with a sudden burst of anemone-like delight. One look at the fisherman though and I could tell that was a bad idea. Those thick plaid sleeves would send me overboard after it.

"Oh please!" she begged.

"No, I can't do that. Let me think…" I rubbed my brow. "I need a different plan."

The foghorn gloomed again.

Out loud I said, "I see you got a crab."

He was intent on the swirls in the air.

I said, "They're hard to catch, I bet. On a line that is."

He glanced at me briefly. "Not if you know what you're doing."

I nodded. "I guess that's true." That was it for my fishing material. I could tell him about the time I hooked a goldfish with a paperclip and lost it. Big deal. I had to try a different tactic. You might say, why not look into this fellow's mind and see what he's thinking and work with that? Not a bad idea, but I was getting nothing from him. Dead air. Then I thought of something. "Say, would you let me buy that crab?"

He turned his weathered face to me and that cigarette blazed.

The crab coughed from the bucket.

I wanted to tell him I was serious, I meant it, but for the moment that glare of his had frozen me.

Everything went back into motion when the fishing pole twitched. He gave the line a swift tug then started to reel in his catch. I watched in silence. The thin filament cut into the fog. We were thirty feet from the water, whatever was on its way bent the rod. We were all holding our breath.

When I could see what was ascending, I thought he had caught an old shoe. Something that tramped over the mud. Then it spread out a pair of yellow spiny fins like bat wings. I don't know what it was, it was the ugliest fish I've ever seen. As it was swung over the railing, rotating on the line, its glossy eyes spotted me and it groused, "What are you looking at?"

The fisherman let it flop to the boards and he put a shoe on its back to hold it tight. My head echoed with an obscene slew of words that culminated with a red explosion as the hook was yanked out of the fish's deformed mouth.

"What is that thing?" I asked.

My new companion puffed, "Dinner." He held it carefully, avoiding the poisonous spines, with the creature's troll face snarling at me.

I won't repeat what it said. I wouldn't want to

put it in print. Like some Alaskan deckhand, it swore horrifically, in ways that are not clever or endearing. It snorted, jeered and blew itself up big as a basketball. Squirming in the man's hands, it gave a sudden thrash of its tail that almost got it free.

The struggling fisherman yelped, "Hold that bucket for me!"

I pictured that weighty monstrosity plopped down on top of my poor crab.

"Get it!"

I jumped. I grabbed for the bucket and my fingers brushed that slick yellow plastic and fumbled with the edge and suddenly it was airborne, off the pier. I can't swear that I did it consciously. I had no time to rejoice, or see it fall, or even hear it splash. Everything happened so fast. And then the fisherman was shrieking, grabbing at his right hand.

With a sickening wet slap, the fish landed on the pier and in that moment, time slowed. One of those unwholesome eyes winked at me. Maybe I could have seized it if I wanted to. There was still a chance for me to act, as it rolled over and dropped back to the sea.

This time I did hear the splash. It was big. Followed by another foghorn wail.

And next to me an animal moaned, an animal that just lost its meal and a two-dollar bucket. His cigarette finally fell. It went down, right through the gap between the boards.

I bumbled with apologies. He was crumpled, clutching his poisoned hand and when his eyes found me, I've never felt such hate. He didn't need to say a word, I knew what he thought of me.

"I'm going to leave," I said. What else could I do. There was no encore.

I was glad his voice faded as I hurried away. What a relief we shared no psychic connection. Honestly, I was lucky I wasn't dumped over the railing too. Funny, then I'd be the one needing a mermaid. What a spectacle.

This is why I don't go chasing telepathy. This is why I stay amateur.

The fog shrouded out where I'd been and where I was going. I was happy to get lost in it, but the inside of my head was abuzz with new voices.

84

9

AGES 0-120

From their sign out front you could say they serve everyone, but I happen to be 121 years old. As of last Tuesday.

I don't know why I put off going there for over a century. I suppose I was busy with other things. And now that it's forbidden to me I feel I must see it, even if it's the last thing I do. There are days I feel that way.

I called for a robot at 7:30 AM. I still make coffee the old-fashioned way and it was percolating on the stove.

I told them, "Good morning, my name is Dottie," and I said I'd like a taxi in an hour. "Thank you very much." Of course I remember when you had a person to talk to. Those were the days. I'm prone to memories, I slide in and out of them all the time.

After finishing my coffee, I brought the cup to the sink and washed it. No sense leaving it for later. The room was quiet. I turned up my hearing aid until I could hear the clock tick on the wall and then the telephone began to ring. I went to where it was waiting.

"Hello, this is Dottie."

"Hello ma'am, this is your Electric Cab. I just arrived."

"Oh, yes. Thank you, I'm on my way." I put on my wool coat, and my blue hat. I usually wait until the day has warmed before I go out.

The house opened the front door and chimed, "See you soon, dear."

That was my husband's voice. On recorded tape. He will greet me again when I get back. He's been gone for a long time but hearing him hidden in the speaker walls makes him seem around.

I leaned on my cane and went into chilly daylight. At the end of the yard, a yellow taxi puttered by the curb. I don't know why I was in such a rush to get there, I could have waited until the afternoon, but when you're 121 you need to get things done. And this was a ride I had waited so long to take.

The portly driver got out and approached. "Would you like assistance, ma'am?"

"No," I smiled. That must have pleased the

robot because it reached in its uniform and got a pack of Camels.

"Smoke?" it offered.

I was taking the last steps to the car. That was effort enough for my lungs. I said, "No thank you very much." I know the driver was just being friendly, but can't a robot tell a 121 year old woman when they see one? My goodness.

"Suit yourself," it shrugged and it stuck a cigarette in its clenched mandible. It stood by the back door as I slowly entered the confines of the taxi. Last time I rode in one of these contraptions, it was pulled by a horse. That's a joke, I'm not that old. I pulled my leg inside and smoothed my coat. "Alright, lady," the robot said, shut the door and went around to the driver's side. Once it got inside, it looked in the rearview mirror and asked, "Where to, lady?"

I told him and he chuckled knowingly. Anyone who goes there is required by law to keep it a secret. All these years and I've heard a lot of rumors and they go all over the place. I think it must be a sort of dreamland that you forget when you wake up.

The robot's eyes were in the mirror again looking at me. "So…ah, where do you fit into the

0-120 scheme, ma'am? That is, if you don't mind telling me."

This robot had no manners at all. But I told him, "I turned one hundred twenty-one last week."

It took a hand off of the steering wheel and wiped a palm across that steely forehead and uttered a long whistle. I looked at the passing buildings. Then it occurred to its clicking mind, "Say, that means you're older than the cutoff! How do you plan on getting in there?"

I clasped my cane. "I plan on reasoning with them. That's the best plan."

It chuckled, "Oh you think so? Listen, I happen to know they follow the book. You know those stuffed-shirt types." It shook its head and wheezed, "Ohhh boy…"

I remember days we used to swim in the Atlantic. My grandparents sat on the shore, under black umbrellas stuck in the sand. I never would have spoken to them like this robot driving me.

My ignoring it didn't matter. It continued, "But when—notice I say when not if—you get the cold shoulder, come back to me. I know a fellah can get you in easy." And it snapped its metal fingers.

Those yellow eyes were still looking at me in the

mirror. I wished it would watch the road. "That's fine, thank you." I had to say.

"You got it," it promised.

Thankfully it returned its attention to the traffic. I got my purse after we passed Food Giant, we were nearly there. The meter was running with numbers. I used to get a cup of coffee for 50 cents. This is the future though, this is when a hundred dollars gets you a five minute ride with a robot.

On the corner of Lincoln Street, the whole block was circled by a tall concrete wall.

The cab turned into the curb right in front of the big words painted on the wall in huge red letters. ALL ARE WELCOME AGES 0-120. At least the robot driver had the decency to get out and lend me a hand. I stood beside a six-foot tall W, right in the middle of the sign, and removed enough credits from my purse.

The driver crumpled its hand around the payment and lowered its voice. "I'll wait right here if you need me, see?"

I nodded and made a tight smile. I had no intention of seeing him again. Ahead of me was a ticket booth next to the gate. I had every intention of being on the other side of the wall soon.

The words on the cement wall crept past me. I stopped at the start of them to catch my breath. Some people milled around, the sort you always see outside an amusement park or a Broadway show. A family hustled by me, their little girls pulling them along. There was no parking along the long stretch of sidewalk, but cars were pulling up and dropping people off. At the end of the block there was a blue tour bus. It was kind of exciting being here. I had to stop a couple more times before I reached the ticket booth. My heart beat like a bird.

When I finally joined the line, I was already tired for the day. I hoped once they let me through, there would be an option for a wheelchair, or a robot wagon. A bench would be good too, maybe I could just sit for a while and let it wash over.

Everyone chattered like sparrows. Their voices sung in and out around me. It buoyed me along to the ticket window. I hung my cane on the ledge and a shadowy person behind the barred window waited while I took my ID out of my purse. "It's my first time here," I smiled.

They seemed delighted to hear that, taking my card, disappearing from sight. I saw a blur of more shadows through the bars.

"Is everything alright?" I called, tilting my head to hear.

Someone else appeared in the window. It wasn't the same teenager who answered me. "There appears to be a problem with your ID, Ms. Renfield."

"Oh dear…"

"Can we just verify your age please? Are you 121?"

I nodded. I told him how I'd been meaning to visit all my life, I just never got around to it until now and I laughed a little as I said it. He wasn't impressed though. It was just like the robot taxi driver warned me. My ID came sliding back to me through the gap. I couldn't believe it. "We've never had to refuse admittance before," the man told me, "but I'm sorry, you'll have to step aside and let the next person through."

"What happened?" a woman behind me asked.

"They won't let me in."

The voice from the window called, "Next!" and I was forgotten as the line pushed ahead.

I wasn't able to get far before I had to lean on my cane. My breath came and went raggedly.

That's how my robot taxi driver found me again. It popped open a wheelchair and urged me to sit down. I didn't need convincing.

"I won't say I told you so," it clucked, "but I told you so."

I was too tired to reply. I could feel the wheels turn and bump over the sidewalk back towards the cab. The robot leaned over my shoulder and promised to get me in the gate. I didn't see how. My eyes shut and I was asleep before I knew it.

The sound of arguing woke me. I was sitting in the cab, brick walls in the windows, we were parked in an alley. In front of the car, two robots were gesturing loudly. One was the driver, the other was a rusted chap wearing a long black overcoat. From their spirited tone I would guess they were doing a bit of dickering. I don't know how long I'd been sleeping or where we were exactly, but I felt rested enough to open the door and join them.

It didn't look like a nice part of town. I pressed my cane into an oily puddle.

Both robots noticed me and stopped chattering and the driver greeted me and the rusty one sputtered, "As I live and breathe…"

"What do you think, Gary?" my cabbie asked

the other robot.

With a whirr, Gary's eye-lens telescoped and gave me the once over. "Sure. I think I can work with her. Come on over here, darling."

We were only separated by the length of the car, but it took me a full minute to get to them. This was a busy day for me. I may be the only one in the city like me, I know I'm a miracle.

"A hundred and twenty one," Gary marveled.

"What can you do for her?" my cabbie asked.

"For starters," Gary said, "I can take off fifty years."

"What?" I asked. My hearing is still pretty good, but I couldn't believe what I heard.

"For a little sugar, I can make you 70 again."

I tapped my ear, "Sugar?"

"Yeah, you know. Kale. Simoleons. Frog skins."

"You mean money?"

"Shhh!" Gary hushed me and looked around suspiciously. "We don't say that word out loud."

"Gary does good work," my cabbie interrupted. "But he doesn't come cheap."

I whispered, "How...What would you do to me?"

Gary promised, "Don't worry, it's painless. I

just give you a simple shot. I can prepare one for you. The years will just drop away."

"It's true," my cabbie said, "I've seen it before."

Gary was quick to continue, "Now, of course it can't last indefinitely. Nothing does. But I can guarantee you it'll last two hours, a little more or less. After that you'll return to your current state. Good news is that gives you plenty of time to get past the gate."

I agreed to the procedure. Why not? Common sense had taken me this far. I was a little taken aback by Gary's fee, but what else was I going to do with my money? I paid and the robots led me back to the taxi where I sat down, while Gary prepared the shot. That black coat had pockets sewn inside, filled with little vials. It didn't take those rusted fingers long.

Gary was right, I didn't feel a thing. Then, as I watched my hands folded on my lap, they transformed. All throughout my body, I could feel that potion at work like mercury bubbling. The world tilted, I shut my eyes, I was falling into years, my life was rushing in reverse. Memories flashed. I tried to slow them down, I tried to grab onto something and finally I did. My hands held onto a long rope I remembered. It was tied to a tree next to a green river and when I was ten, I used to swing on it and let go. It stretched with me until it grew taut and I stopped. I kept my eyes closed though. I could hear those two robots bickering.

The cabbie barked, "You call that 70?"

"A slight overdose," said Gary.

And that's when I opened my eyes.

Phone
Phone
ELEVEN

10.

PRECOGNITION

Harold got that feeling again as he approached the cashier. He knew what was going to happen. It wasn't a movie of the future that played in his mind, it was a sudden crumpled warning that twisted in his chest. He knew the place would be robbed, and soon. He quickly paid for his iced tea and hurried outside to the payphone. He didn't know exactly how much time he had, but there were no other customers inside and no one approaching the doors. Could be minutes, could be an hour. He dialed the police station and waited for Carol to answer.

'The Wizard' is what they called Harold. Only lately he didn't feel that way. Three times in a row he'd been wrong. The police department had become disenchanted. Carol's tone said it all. "Where are you?"

"The 7-Eleven on Morris."

"Okay," she said. "I'll send someone," and then she added, "I really hope you're right this time, Harold."

He hoped so too. He never had this trouble before. Was he losing his touch?

A city bus rumbled by. People were always going somewhere. Maybe his gift of precognition had picked up and left too. No, he still felt it in him. Something was going to happen.

He was sitting on the bench next to the payphone, drinking his tea, when the police cruiser steered onto the lot and parked in front of him. Two officers sat on the front seat. Harold knew them from the last time. It didn't go well last time at the Chevron station. They read Harold the riot act that day. And here they were again, arriving at a peaceful convenience store.

Harold stood as they left their car. He screwed the cap back on his tea and waved at them.

Lieutenant Deevers got close, close enough to spear Harold with the toothpick clenched in his mouth. "This the scene of the crime, Wizard?" Beside him, his partner chuckled.

Harold assured them this was the place. It might

look calm, but a robbery was going to happen. It was predestined, someone was going to do it. They stared at Howard skeptically, but before this recent run of bad luck, they had witnessed his predictions come true. It was crazy, they could be standing outside a business or a bank or a store just like now and the perpetrator would walk right past them in a trance on a path to crime. All they had to do was step in behind and stop it. But that seemed like ages ago.

Deevers chewed the toothpick and looked over Harold's shoulder, through the 7-Eleven window. A kid was staring at the candy shelf. The cashier was slumped over *The Herald*. "What do you think, Parks? Should we call for reinforcements?"

Parks chuckled again.

"Shoot..." Deevers turned on Harold, "If you're wasting our time again—" but his words stopped as a man—oblivious of the cruiser, the two cops and Harold—limped past them, pushed on the door and went inside. Deevers and Parks followed him. Harold watched from where he was, outside. As the man stopped in front of the register and reached in his coat pocket, Harold had already seen him taking out a gun.

That isn't what happened though. Deevers and Parks weren't expecting what happened either. When they lunged and seized the man's arm and wrestled it behind his back, a crumpled dollar bill fell to the floor.

"What are you doing?" the man cried, "I was just getting change for the telephone!"

Harold heard that from outside. He saw the dollar and the wholly unexpected reality unfolding. Fortunately he couldn't hear the two policemen explain the mistake they had made. The kid with the candy bar watched in a sort of shock. Harold had seen enough. He left his spot by the window and stepped off the curb and hurried from the 7-Eleven. When he was almost to the chain link fence ending the lot, he heard Deever's voice shout at him from the store.

"You're through Wizard!"

"That's right!" Parks piped in, "Keep running!"

Harold didn't even realize he was running. He made himself stop and he tried to turn at the fence like someone just out for a stroll. It didn't take a mind reader to know his work with the city was done. His signals were mixed up. What was going on with them? The beaten path meandered into brush and when he was hidden from the parking lot, he stopped to lean against a tree. He was dizzy. Sometimes the psychic radio is just that, a nervous spin that dies like a top. He hoped not.

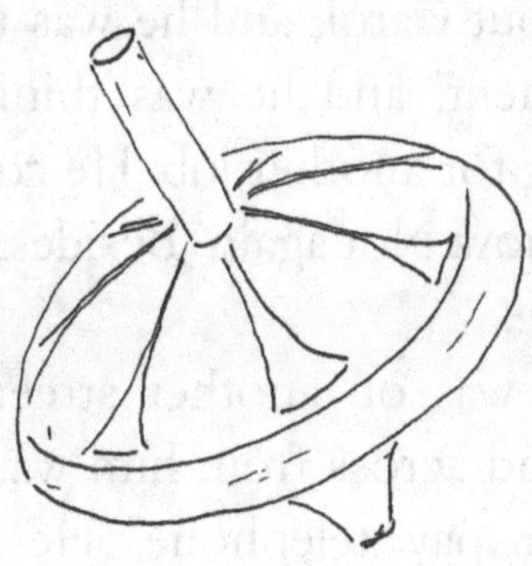

Carol would be disappointed. He knew that. She wanted to believe he had magical powers. Turns out he was just like everyone else. The path took him along a shallow stream. Lots of green ferns, moss, bare branches starting to bud with new leaves. It was a miniature forest between Morris and Page Street. Usually it calmed Harold to walk through but not now, today he was like a werewolf limping through the snapping underbrush. The birds must have sensed his distress. A junco alarm went off in an alder.

When the woods ran out, he was facing the back of an apartment building complex. A gutter hung loose off the roof, the rain had stained the eaves. No sign of life in the dark windows. The path went past a broken barbeque. He was thinking about Carol, and he was thinking about the department, and he was thinking he better start looking for another job. He couldn't go back to the sideshow. Not again. Besides, he burned his bridges there.

Soon he was on another street, parked with more cars and across from him was a gas station, and another pay telephone. He was glad the phonebooth was in the parking lot, well away from the store. He didn't want to get too close to it, he couldn't risk another premonition. Sunoco was on its own if it happened.

Carol had a desk in the corner. The window looked out on a gray lot filled with department cars and vans. When her phone rang, she knew it was Harold.

"Hi Carol," he said.

"Harold!"

"I'm sorry," he began woefully. "I don't know what's happened to me, I—"

"Harold!" she chirped, "Listen to me. You weren't wrong about the robbery. It happened just like you said, same time, only it was at a different 7-Eleven—it was the one on Belmont."

"Belmont?"

She continued, "I did a little research and found out those other times you had it wrong, there were robberies in different places too, exactly when you predicted. You're just wrong about the scene of the crime, that's all."

"That's all," he repeated.

"Don't you get it, Harold? This is good news. Once you figure out why your directions are going wrong and get it fixed, we're back in the ballgame."

Harold wasn't so sure.

Carol said, "My guess is triangulation. It happens to homing pigeons sometimes. Atmospheric conditions can be a factor too. Or maybe…" and her voice dropped confidentially, "You're being jammed. Someone could be deliberately falsifying your reading."

Harold was about to respond, but his dime had no more to give and there were no more coins in his pockets. He felt a dollar bill, but he didn't dare go into the Sunoco and ask for change. That would be tempting fate and he already saw how that played out. He returned the phone to its cradle and started to wander. That's how he went about his day—exploring the streets, going in and out of astral planes—and that's how he used to be paid. Now it was just habit.

Carol gave him something to think about. It never occurred to him that his talents could be jammed. If someone was interfering, who were they? He stopped at the bench in front of a laundromat so he could search his mind. Like a Buddha, he folded his hands and shut his eyes. The air around him swam with the sound of traffic and the vivid florid aroma of laundry soap. Harold drifted along further from shore. A shark circled him, brushing aside the darkness.

"Hello Harry. Long time no see."

When he opened his eyes, she smiled.

"Charlotte," he said. It's true, it had been a very long time. She had been waiting for this meeting. And just like that, he knew it was her doing, baffling him. She always did have that power over him. He could also tell she was doing alright these days— tailored sleek as a Hollywood star with jewels on her hands and a pearl necklace—she wasn't working for the police department that was for sure. She told him with a look what she wanted. She would cloud his mind if he tried to report another crime in progress, but together, imagine what they could do.

The RETURN of the DIAL

He was the first person I've seen wearing a suit in five million years. I watched him approach, hoping a saber-tooth wouldn't get him before he got to me. Into the tree line, up the hill, he clambered over the rocks and moss. Shoes wouldn't be invented until Mesopotamia. I don't know when the first paisley tie was invented. He waved a hand at the giant dragonfly circling him. I've got used to them. I've been here five years.

"Hello!" I called down to him. I always knew they'd find me. Took them long enough though! For five years I've been living in a cave on the southside of a pile of rocks. For five long years, okay…Imagine that—the Pleistocene!—no, you have no idea. It's a miracle I'm still here, that's all I'm going to say.

I still wasn't sure he was from Ready Now, but that's what I guessed, that's what I've been waiting for all this time, that someone from their company would hear about my misadventure and come looking for me. When he was near enough I could recognize the RN logo sewn to the pocket of his coat, I yelled again. If you pray long enough, it might come true.

I left the cave and went out to meet him. Sometimes the sloths would give you a chase, but it didn't take much to get away. For me, that is. I know my way around. I worried this guy might be easy prey. And imagine him coming all this eternity only to die.

Ten feet from me he stopped and asked, "Are you Ned Fedders?"

What did he think I would say? It was such a strange thing to ask the one modern person stuck in this prehistoric land. What if I wasn't Ned Fedders? What if I was someone else who by some mistake dropped through time like a stone? Did they have a checklist?

He looked past me at my cave, "Is there a Ned Fedders who lives here?"

"Yes!" I shouted. It had been so long since I

spoke to someone, I felt like a madman. My only friends were animals and the orange birds I call crows. "Sorry, yes. I'm Ned Fedders. I'm sorry, I didn't know what to say."

"Oh good!" He took another step. "How are you?"

"I'm fine."

"Wonderful!" He didn't waste any time. He reached in his suit and got a letter out of a pocket. "Can we have your agreement that you won't talk about this unfortunate accident of yours? We just need your signature right here."

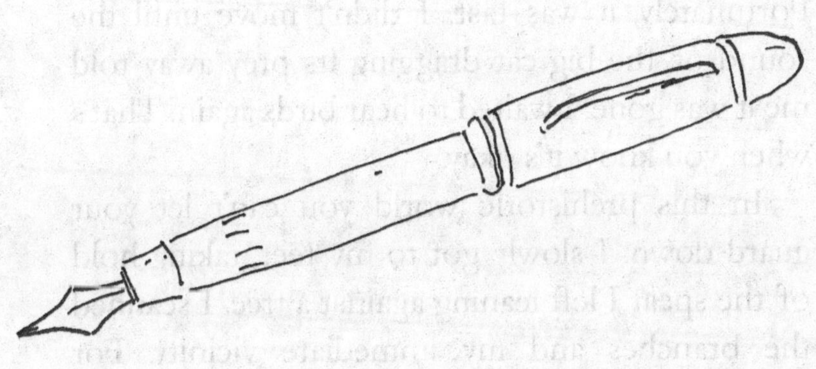

"My signature?" I asked.

"Yes, then I can bring you back." He patted his suit pocket where he told me he kept his time machines, one for himself and one for me.

I laughed. "You don't want me to tell anyone where I've been all this time?"

"They won't even know. I'll bring you back to the exact moment you originally left."

I couldn't believe it. I laughed again and had to sit down on a stone. That's probably what saved my life. The tiger had been waiting for the right moment to strike from the branch just over my head. A giant blur of fur. It hit my visitor in the chest and down they went, scattering rocks. I lay flat against the ground. It was all over for him. Fortunately, it was fast. I didn't move until the sound of the big cat dragging its prey away told me it was gone. I waited to hear birds again. That's when you know it's okay.

In this prehistoric world you can't let your guard down. I slowly got to my feet, taking hold of the spear I left leaning against a tree. I scanned the branches and my immediate vicinity. For now I was alright. But ahead of me the turf was disrupted, clawed and bloodied. A sudden deadly strike. My time travel rescuer was gone.

It was too good to be true. Imagine, me reappearing in the 21st century in these caveman rags. Believe it or not, I laughed again. You have to be able to laugh, even as I approached the awful site of the attack. Then it occurred to me I still had a chance to return to America. I remembered he had his time machines in his suit pocket. There was blood and more blood as the tiger pulled its meal through the rubble and weeds. After five years here, I wasn't shocked by the sight.

Some pocket change littered the trail. I didn't need it. We didn't have vending machines here. As I followed, I kept my spear ready, and I scanned the ground on either side of me for more traces of civilized society. I found a coffee shop punch card. I quickly picked that up and examined it. He only needed one more purchase for a free coffee. How cruel fate can be. I put it in my fur carry bag. If I got out of here, I could use it, raise a cup and toast a fossil that lay under the city's concrete.

Tracking a saber-tooth tiger with its fresh kill is foolhardy, but I was forging on, I needed that time machine. A shoe rested awkwardly in the yellow flowers. An expensive leather shoe with tassels. It didn't interest me. I'm way past shoes. I didn't want the gold watch either. One of those orange crows would find it and carry it to its nest.

Through the trees to my left, I could see a giant sloth. I say giant, but this is the age when *everything* is giant and mostly ferocious. Even that flower I saw the shoe laying on. It would be consuming that loafer by now, tassel and all. I have never got close enough to a tiger to use a spear, I wouldn't want to try. I have learned to walk almost silently.

I saw something else you don't want to know about, then spotted in the ferns a shredded part of his suit jacket. With no arm in it, the sleeve hung over a broken branch. I reached for it with the spear and hooked it free. The coat was torn down the center, but I had the half I needed, the part that had a pocket sewn to the lining. I hurried my hand into that silk and felt the slim shapes of two time machines. His was personalized, emblazoned with his name and a swatch of gold enamel. The other device was a standard Ready Now. The dial was already set and I didn't wait another second before I pressed the red button.

And the next thing I knew, I was standing at the edge of the school parking lot. It was the same scene I left five million years ago. It was sunny, there were telephone wires overhead. My daughter was being comforted by the teacher. There she was! I stomped across the gravel, kicking little bits of stone with my fur shoes. For a second, I thought the car that almost hit me was a wooly rhinoceros. She looked up at the blared sound of the horn and saw me. I dropped my spear, I didn't need it anymore, and I ran to her.

The *WIRES* and *CIRCUITS* of *EARTH*
Written during Winter into Spring 2022

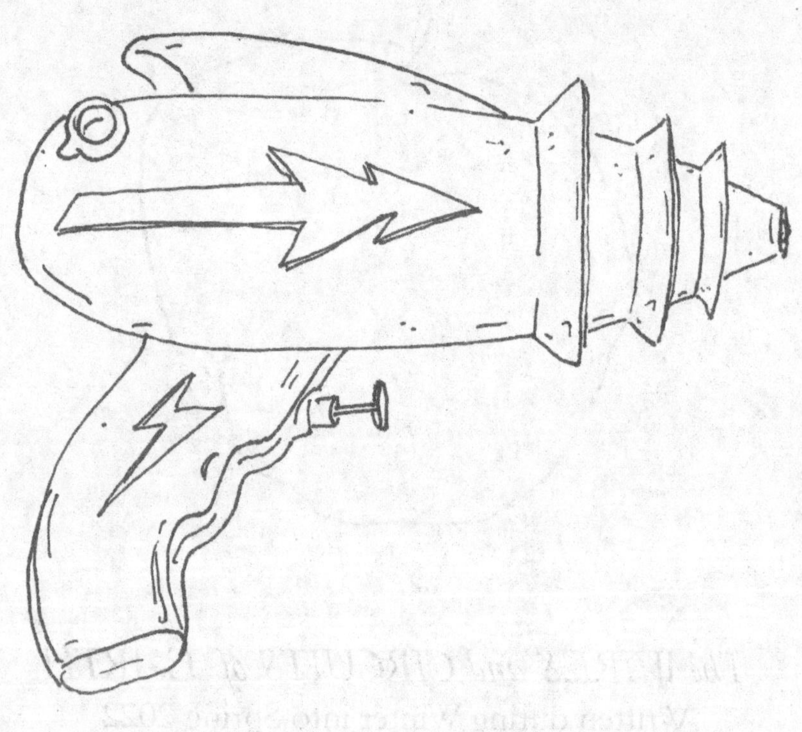

Illustration from *The Trillium Witch* (2021)

Books by Good Deed Rain

Saint Lemonade, Allen Frost, 2014. Two novels illustrated by the author in the manner of the old Big Little Books.

Playground, Allen Frost, 2014. Poems collected from seven years of chapbooks.

Roosevelt, Allen Frost, 2015. A Pacific Northwest novel set in July, 1942, when a boy and a girl search for a missing elephant. Illustrated throughout by Fred Sodt.

5 Novels, Allen Frost, 2015. Novels written over five years, featuring circus giants, clockwork animals, detectives and time travelers.

The Sylvan Moore Show, Allen Frost, 2015. A short story omnibus of 193 stories written over 30 years.

Town in a Cloud, Allen Frost, 2015. A three-part book of poetry, written during the Bellingham rainy seasons of fall, winter, and spring.

A Flutter of Birds Passing Through Heaven: A Tribute to Robert Sund, 2016. Edited by Allen Frost and Paul Piper. The story of a legendary Ish River poet & artist.

At the Edge of America, Allen Frost, 2016. Two novels in one book blend time travel in a mythical poetic America.

Lake Erie Submarine, Allen Frost, 2016. A two week vacation in Ohio inspired these poems, illustrated by the author.

and Light, Paul Piper, 2016. Poetry written over three years. Illustrated with watercolors by Penny Piper.

The Book of Ticks, Allen Frost, 2017. A giant collection of 8 mysterious adventures featuring Phil Ticks. Illustrated throughout by Aaron Gunderson.

I Can Only Imagine, Allen Frost, 2017. Five adventures of love and heartbreak dreamed in an imaginary world. Cover & color illustrations by Annabelle Barrett.

The Orphanage of Abandoned Teenagers, Allen Frost, 2017. A fictional guide for teens and their parents. Illustrated by the author.

In the Valley of Mystic Light: An Oral History of the Skagit Valley Arts Scene, 2017. A comprehensive illustrated tribute. Edited by Claire Swedberg & Rita Hupy.

Different Planet, Allen Frost, 2017. Four science fiction adventures: reincarnation, robots, talking animals, outer space and clones. Illustrated by Laura Vasyutynska.

Go with the Flow: A Tribute to Clyde Sanborn, 2018. Edited by Allen Frost. The life and art of a timeless river poet. In beautiful living color!

Homeless Sutra, Allen Frost, 2018. Four stories: Sylvan Moore, a flying monk, a water salesman, and a guardian rabbit.

The Lake Walker, Allen Frost 2018. A little novel set in black and white like one of those old European movies about death and life.

A Hundred Dreams Ago, Allen Frost, 2018. A winter book of poetry and prose. Illustrated by Aaron Gunderson.

Almost Animals, Allen Frost, 2018. A collection of linked stories, thinking about what makes us animals.

The Robotic Age, Allen Frost, 2018. A vaudeville magician and his faithful robot track down ghosts. Illustrated throughout by Aaron Gunderson.

Kennedy, Allen Frost, 2018. This sequel to *Roosevelt* is a coming-of-age fable set during two weeks in 1962 in a mythical Kennedyland. Illustrated throughout by Fred Sodt.

Fable, Allen Frost, 2018. There's something going on in this country and I can best relate it in fable: the parable of the rabbits, a bedtime story, and the diary of our trip to Ohio.

Elbows & Knees: Essays & Plays, Allen Frost, 2018. A thrilling collection of writing about some of my favorite subjects, from B-movies to Brautigan.

The Last Paper Stars, Allen Frost 2019. A trip back in time to the 20 year old mind of Frankenstein, and two other worlds of the future.

Walt Amherst is Awake, Allen Frost, 2019. The dreamlife of an office worker. Illustrated throughout by Aaron Gunderson.

When You Smile You Let in Light, Allen Frost, 2019. An atomic love story written by a 23 year old.

Pinocchio in America, Allen Frost, 2019. After 82 years buried underground, Pinocchio returns to life behind a car repair shop in America.

Taking Her Sides on Immortality, Robert Huff, 2019. The long awaited poetry collection from a local, nationally renowned master of words.

Florida, Allen Frost, 2019. Three days in Florida turned into a book of sunshine inspired stories.

Blue Anthem Wailing, Allen Frost, 2019. My first novel written in college is an apocalyptic, Old Testament race through American shadows while Amelia Earhart flies overhead.

The Welfare Office, Allen Frost, 2019. The animals go in and out of the office, leaving these stories as footprints.

Island Air, Allen Frost, 2019. A detective novel featuring haiku, a lost library book and streetsongs.

Imaginary Someone, Allen Frost, 2020. A fictional memoir featuring 45 years of inspirations and obstacles in the life of a writer.

Violet of the Silent Movies, Allen Frost, 2020. A collection of starry-eyed short story poems, illustrated by the author.

The Tin Can Telephone, Allen Frost, 2020. A childhood memory novel set in 1975 Seattle, illustrated by author.

Heaven Crayon, Allen Frost, 2020. How the author's first book *Ohio Trio* would look if printed as a Big Little Book. Illustrated by the author.

Old Salt, Allen Frost, 2020. Authors of a fake novel get chased by tigers. Illustrations by the author.

A Field of Cabbages, Allen Frost, 2020. The sequel to *The Robotic Age* finds our heroes in a race against time to save Sunny Jim's ghost. Illustrated by Aaron Gunderson.

River Road, Allen Frost, 2020. A paperboy delivers the news to a ghost town. Illustrated by the author.

The Puttering Marvel, Allen Frost, 2021. Eleven short stories with illustrations by the author.

Something Bright, Allen Frost, 2021. 106 short story poems walking with you from winter into spring. Illustrated by the author.

The Trillium Witch, Allen Frost, 2021. A detective novel about witches in the Pacific Northwest rain. Illustrated by the author.

Cosmonaut, Allen Frost, 2021. Yuri Gagarin's rocket lands in America. Midnight jazz, folk music, mystery and sorcery. Illustrated by the author.

Thriftstore Madonna, Allen Frost, 2021. 124 summer story poems. Illustrated by the author.

Half a Giraffe, Allen Frost, 2021. A magical novel about a counterfeiter and his unusual, beloved pet. Illustrated by the author.

Lexington Brown & The Pond Projector, Allen Frost, 2022. An underwater invention takes three friends through time. Illustrated by Aaron Gunderson.

The Robert Huck Museum, Allen Frost, 2022. The artist's life story told in photographs, woodcuts, paintings, prints and drawings.

Mrs. Magnusson & Friends, Allen Frost, 2022. A collection of 13 stories featuring mystery and ginkgo leaves.

Magic Island, Allen Frost, 2022. There's a memory machine in this magical novel that takes us to college.

A Red Leaf Boat, Allen Frost, 2022. Inspired by Japan, this book of 142 poems is the result of walking in autumn.

Forest & Field, Allen Frost, 2022. 117 forest and field recordings made during the summer months, ending with a lullaby.

The Wires and Circuits of Earth, Allen Frost, 2022. 11 stories from a train station pulp magazine.

Last
Exit
free